LUCKED

ANGEL DEVLIN

CONTENTS

Chapter 1	1
Chapter 2	9
Chapter 3	21
Chapter 4	27
Chapter 5	33
Chapter 6	43
Chapter 7	49
Chapter 8	61
Chapter 9	73
Chapter 10	81
Chapter 11	91
Chapter 12	103
Chapter 13	107
Epilogue	111
About the Author	113
Also by Angel Devlin	115

No part of this book may be reproduced or transmitted in any form or by any means, electronic or mechanical, including photocopying, recording or by any information storage and retrieval system without the written permission of the author, except for the use of brief quotations in a book review.

Copyright (c) 2018 by Angel Devlin
All rights reserved.

To my sister Maz.
For joining in with the insanity, when I said 'let's f**k off to Dublin', and gave you 3 days notice.

To Kelsey Burns
My #SFAM

For a trip to Dublin, filled with laughter, that I'll never forget!

CHAPTER One

You before me

Anna

"It was supposed to be our wedding next."

Attending the wedding of my colleague, Rachel, and her new husband, Evan, I couldn't help but whine. After carrying on a Love/Hate relationship for years, my fellow barmaid and the love of her life had lost all common sense, got engaged after one day, and married after ten months.

My own fiance, Chris, sighed and wrinkled his nose. It irritated me when he did that. I wanted to punch him in it.

"Our wedding's in July. You can't expect other people to wait until ours has taken place. Was Rachel supposed to check with you before booking the hotel?" He forced a laugh, but I knew in reality he was getting fed up of my impatience at becoming Mrs Mellon.

"I'm sorry. I can't wait for it to be our day that's all."

Because it took so fucking long for you to propose in the first place.

Chris and I had been together for six years and had met via mutual friends, Jenny and Kian. I had gone to school with Jenny and Chris played football with Kian.

At twenty-eight, I was well ready to get that gold band on my finger and those babies on the way. I wanted at least two, and my biological clock was ticking. Chris was thirty-two, and being a typical bloke, didn't see what the rush was.

He'd eventually proposed at Jenny and Kian's wedding two years ago. By then I'd wondered if it was ever going to happen to be honest. I think my family had thought the same, judging by their stupefied faces when we'd announced our engagement.

But it had. Jenny had thrown the bouquet, and it had landed firmly in my manicured hands. Of course I had the advantage of my school netball training, honed in adulthood on the basketball game at the seaside slots, and my threats to kidnap her firstborn if I didn't get it.

But I'd not quite expected my proposal to be a drunken man slurring, "So I suppose I should put a ring on it," just as Beyonce's 'Single Ladies' finished, a song I'd given my all too. After six years though, that's how things went, kind of casual and comfortable. We weren't like Evan and Rachel all goo-goo eyed. Chris and I farted in front of each other freely (he did mostly. I did revenge farts), and stayed home with a takeaway, rather than getting dressed up for dates. It was settled. Familiar.

I stole a sidelong look at his bored face. Blokes didn't get weddings, did they? It would be different when it was our own, and he saw me, a vision in white, walking down the aisle towards him. He'd have a more active role then.

"I now pronounce you husband and wife."

A tear rolled down my cheek as I stared at the utter love and devotion on Rachel and Evan's faces, and when told he could now kiss his bride, Evan tipped her back and gave her a movie star kiss. I made a note to ask Chris to do something similar when it was our turn.

Then they left the hotel room to everyone's cheers.

"Thank fuck. Can I get a pint now?" Chris asked me.

I rolled my eyes. "No, it's the photos yet. Then the toast. We drink champagne with them."

"Am I in hell?" Chris asked. "Did I die and I don't know? Like in that film with Bruce Willis?"

I nudged him with my elbow. "Behave yourself."

By the time of the evening reception my fiance was in a much better mood with a couple of pints and some buffet food down him. He dragged me onto the dance floor for a bit of his dad-style dancing. This is what I loved about him. He could be the life and soul of a party. As we danced, Rachel joined the dance floor with a couple of bridesmaids. I glanced at her lacy, white dress. She looked like a princess.

"I know I said this already, but you look beautiful." I shouted over the music.

"Thank you." She shouted back.

"Your wedding was perfect. Mine next!"

"Yeah, it was perfect once Evan understood that he wasn't writing his vows on disposable cards." She giggled.

I laughed back. Evan had proposed in the Nag's Head using the Bob Dylan/INXS/Love Actually style of writing on pieces of white card. I could just imagine his lips pouting at not being able to do that on their special day.

I tried not to take offence that she'd not responded to it being my wedding next. After all this was her day, and if someone tried to overshadow mine, I'd poke them in the eye. So with a smile, I turned back to Chris and carried on bopping away until the lights went up and the reception was over.

In the taxi on the way home, Chris kept trying to

sneak his hand up my dress while he nibbled at my ear.

"I fucking love you. Blow me."

"Ssh." I admonished him, looking over at the taxi driver to see if he'd made out Chris's slurred words.

"Will you suck my cock when we get home? You've not done it in forever. My trousersnake is feeling very lonely. I want to shoot my load down your throat."

He tilted his hips up. I covered my heated red cheeks with my hands as embarrassment burst like a ripe tomato over my face. There was no way the taxi driver hadn't heard that.

Chris sat back and closed his eyes and by the time the cab pulled up outside our rented home, he was making snoring sounds that sounded dreadful, really loud and nasally.

I prodded him awake and paid the taxi driver, apologising for his rude mouth. The driver shrugged and said he'd heard far worse. I opened Chris' door and helped him out. Then I closed it and stood behind him watching as he staggered up the path like a newly walking toddler.

As he reached our front door he span towards me, "You're so fucking hot, Tania. I'm gonna shag you senseless when I get you in the house."

I sighed. He was always mixing up my name with that of his childhood best friend. Good job I'd known her for years now and knew she thought of him as a brother.

"Come on, Casanova. Let's get you a coffee." While he leaned against the wall, I stalked past him to open the door. He staggered inside and managed to faceplant the couch. By the time I'd removed my coat and shoes, and put the kettle on, he was snoring again.

While Chris slept off his hangover the next morning, I fired up my laptop and caught up with Facebook. My friend, Lesley, had sent me a message.

Have you sorted your hen night yet?

I sighed. I'd been trying to think of where we could go for weeks now. With how much a wedding cost, I didn't have much of a budget, and I didn't want to go too far away either. At the same time, I wanted it to be somewhere we'd remember.

I opened a new tab and typed in popular destinations for hen nights.

Blackpool - hell no.

Benidorm - absolutely not.

And then in the sidebar on the page I was visiting I saw a January sale ad for Dublin mini-breaks. I loved Guinness! I clicked through and the prices were nothing short of a miracle. After checking capacity, I sent the link to my mate.

Two days later and it was all booked. What a stroke of luck that had appeared on the page! Another part of my upcoming wedding was organised. It would seem I'd already been given the luck of the Irish!

CHAPTER Two

Hen do? Hen don't.

Anna - March 2018

The four of us did the lazy journey down the travelator to make our way to the Departure Gate of Terminal Three, Manchester airport. There was Lesley; Jenny; and Lesley's sister, Susan, and me. I didn't have a wide circle of friends as I spent most of my time watching TV with Chris. Lesley was an ex-barmaid from the Nag's, and a great laugh.

The morning had already been fantastic. We'd checked in online the day before, so once we were through security, we'd passed through Duty Free where we sampled some free gin. From there I found out that Lesley had booked us all into the lounge and so we breakfasted like kings and drank copious amounts of wine and Guinness even though it was still only eight am.

In true traditional style, I wore a bride-to-be sash and had a condom tied around my neck. We all wore pink cowgirl hats. I wore a tee stating bride, and the others said Bride's Bitches. I was touched that they'd gone to all this effort for me.

Susan had recently got divorced, so she'd been well up for the idea of a weekend away. "I am so gonna pull, lasses. I've had everything waxed in prep."

Typical girly giggle snorts and cackles of laughter were the order of the flight where we celebrated the fact there were no small children aboard and had friendly banter with a group of guys on a stag do.

The flight in itself only took forty minutes. No sooner was the plane up in the air, the pilot was announcing our descent. There hadn't even been enough time for the hostess to reach our seats with the refreshment trolley. Once off the plane, we made our way to the exit and the taxi rank and were dropped off at the entrance to our hotel, The Gresham.

"Wow. Look at this place. I can't believe you got us such a bargain. It's so grand." Jenny looked around her as she dragged her chestnut-coloured hair back off her face. She was being wind whipped.

"Let's get unloaded and then get loaded." Lesley

said in the typical Lesley way. I'd bet Dan's profits at the bar had risen since she left, let's put it that way.

The receptionist at the hotel had advised us to head to the bottom of the road and turn right to find a good bar called The Arlington. With Jenny nominated as the 'Entertainment Manager', the rest of us followed her until we found the place. It had an open front so you could sit among the heaters and it appeared they offered a decent food menu. The pub was like Doctor Who's Tardis—larger on the inside—it seemed to go on for miles! Then again it could have been the fact I'd already walked my daily Fitbit steps around the massive airport and now from the hotel to the pub.

Once we reached the front of the bar, Lesley yelled, "Tequila shots," and that was the start of us girls going wild.

"Fuck, I love this place. My hen night is the best... EVER." I swung my hips to the beat in Copper's, a nightclub we'd finally ended up in. It had a cocktail bar and an endless supply of cocktails had been consumed. I was—to put it mildly—pissed as a fart, and dancing with anyone who was willing. My beer goggles were unable to tell a loser from the most good-looking man in Ireland at that moment in time.

"Oh, I can't wait for your wedding." Jenny yelled over the music. "I feel like Paul O'Grady on Blind Date cos I helped get you two together."

"I think Chris is a dickhead." Lesley said, collapsing in a fit of giggles.

"I'm glad I'm single, all men are dickheads." Chimed in Susan, although five minutes before she'd been doing tonsil-tennis with a so-called 'dickhead'.

"Lesley. That's my future husband you're insulting." I said pouting.

"Yeah, there's still time to call it off."

I laughed and carried on dancing.

"Ooooh, It's Justin Timberlake." I screamed to no one in particular as 'Filthy' started playing. I attempted my own version of a moonwalk, but my feet were sticking to the floor with the spilled alcohol.

"Hey, pretty lady, ya wanna dance?"

I looked up from my feet, trying to locate where the gorgeous Irish accent was coming from. It took me a moment to focus in on the man standing in front of me, and then I stopped dancing, because this man appeared to be fit as fuck.

I touched him. Pressing my hand against different parts of his abdomen. "Are you really very, very handsome and sexy, or is it all the alcohol I've drunk, making you look that way?"

He laughed, revealing the loveliest smile and

neat, white teeth. His hair was light brown, and he had a light dusting of stubble to his chin. He was wearing a jacket, which I could see by the way it kept fluttering open as he danced, was hiding a hot body if the tight white shirt underneath, and my wandering hands weren't lying. It pressed against his chest and I was jealous. My body wanted to be his shirt.

I flapped at the lapels of his jacket. "Aren't you hot? You should take your clothes off."

"You're a bit forward aren't ya? At least buy me a drink first."

It took me several minutes to process what he was saying as he talked so fast, and then I burst out laughing. I found I couldn't stop. Oh fucking hell, this guy was so hilarious.

"So what are you doing here in Dublin?" He asked.

I waved my ring under his face. "I'm getting married in July. This is my last hurrah."

He took a step back. "Oh. That's grand. Congratulations. Well, I'll leave you to your friends. Good luck with t'wedding" He said, and he started to walk away. He pronounced his Th's like 'tuh'. It was so cute. I wanted him to chat to me all night long.

"Stop right there." I yelled, and then I grabbed his arm. "This is my last night of freedom. I want a snog." I yelled again trying to be heard over the music, and I launched myself at him.

Fuck he was good at kissing. In the back of my mind was the fact I was being very badly behaved. I'd never so much as flirted with another guy since being with Chris, but right now I didn't care. I'd caught Chris flirting with other women many a time. It didn't mean anything. Okay, so I was going a bit further than that with my tongue tangling with this other guy's, but I was about to commit to Chris for the rest of my life.

THE. REST. OF. MY. LIFE.

I broke off the kiss. "Excuse me." I said holding my mouth.

Then I ran off to the toilet to throw up.

I sat on the floor of the bathroom, my head resting on the cool wall of the toilet stall, while I tried not to think about what might be on it. Sweat poured from my forehead.

"Anna, you in here?" Jenny's voice bellowed out.

I waved my hand under the gap at the bottom of the door and just groaned.

"Okay. I'll wait here near the sink. Let me know if you need me."

I turned my hand, giving her a thumbs up, before a fresh layer of sweat broke out over my face and I found myself hugging the toilet bowl once again.

After what felt like hours, I managed to make my

way out of the stall. "Can we go back to the hotel now? I need my bed."

"Sure. Let me get the others and let them know."

We were sharing a family room and had set ground rules about whoever came in last being quiet if the others were asleep though none of us had expected that to be the case. We'd been determined to stay out all night, saying goodbye to my single life.

"You sure she's not going to puke, because there's a fine if she does?" The taxi driver warned.

"I've given her a carrier bag. You have my solemn vow that she hasn't been sick for the last fifteen minutes, and if she does it will all go in the bag. We're only at the Gresham."

"Jenny." I said in a whiny voice. "I've got to spend the rest of my life with Chris. Why didn't I have loads more boyfriends before him? I'm twenty-eight. If I live to one hundred, that's, that's..." My brain wouldn't do the sums. "...a million years with the same man."

She placed a hand on my shoulder. "You're getting cold feet, sweetie. Totally natural just before the wedding."

I took a deep sigh of relief. "Oh, thank God. I thought I was having second thoughts. Did you have cold feet?"

"No, I knew Kian was the absolute love of my life."

"Chris is a dickhead."

"Why do you keep saying that, Lesley?"

"Erm, because I think he's a dickhead?" She fastened her seatbelt, and I was totally impressed that she managed it on her first attempt.

"Yeah, but whhhyyy?"

"Let me see - he flirts with other women all the time, belittles you in front of everyone, and I don't believe he's just friends with that Tania." She looked out of the window as the taxi set off.

"Lesley!" Her sister's mouth dropped open.

"Oh, fuck it. I know I said I wouldn't say anything but if I don't do it before the wedding, I won't be able to live with myself. If you go ahead and marry him now, Anna, my conscience is clear."

This was all too much for my drink-addled brain. Had Lesley really just said that about Chris? Or was I in an alcohol-induced coma?

I decided to lean back and close my eyes and worry about it all at a later date.

I vaguely remembered being steered to the hotel room. It faced the front of the hotel. Staggering to the window, I looked out over the shops and the taxi rank seeing people still out enjoying themselves, while I attempted to sober myself up. Jenny had made me a coffee. Lesley and Susan had parked themselves at the hotel bar, not quite ready to call it a night.

My phone rang, and I watched as Jenny grabbed it out of my bag.

"It's Chris."

"Awwww, my baby has rung me."

Chris was out on his own stag do back home in Sheffield. He'd said he couldn't be arsed with organising going away anywhere. To be honest, he didn't have many friends, and even though I knew Tania well, I wouldn't have been happy about him taking his best mate away with him, so it had suited me fine. Plus, it meant more money for the wedding itself.

I pressed the answer button.

"Hello, beautiful fiance."

"Oh baby, yes. Suck on it just like that."

I laughed. "Chris, I can't have phone sex with you! I'm sharing a room with Jenny, you loon."

Then I heard a female voice, one I recognised well.

"Does she do it as good as I do, babe?"

"Fuck, no. If I'd known you could give head like that, I'd have been with you. Oooh yeaah, baby."

I sat back against my headboard, feeling the blood draining from my face.

"What's wrong?" Jenny rushed over.

I gulped and put the phone on loudspeaker.

"Are you still going to marry her?" Tania's voice echoed in the room.

"Oh you know I've got to now, babe. The arrangements have gone too far. It's all happening in July."

"Well, then there's no point in me doing this, is there?"

"No. Don't stop. Okay, darling. I will. I'll call it off. Please put your mouth back on me."

"I'm gonna put more than my mouth around you now."

"Oh, fucking hell, Tan. I forgot how tight you are."

Jenny gasped.

"Oh yeah, baby, yeah, ride me, just like that."

"Turn it off."

"No." I shook my head, determined to listen to the very end. To gain as much information as I could.

When they reached their peak together, I sat rubbing my forehead as if I could dislodge this nightmare from my brain. Was I still drunk? Dreaming? I'd got to still be in that alcohol-coma.

I smacked myself in the cheek. "Ow." I yelled out. That had hurt. Well, I was definitely still awake.

There was a silence and then an "Oh shit."

"What's the matter?" Tania asked.

"Anna?" Chris' voice boomed around the hotel room.

I swiped the phone up from the bed.

"Hello, Chris."

"Anna. I must have accidentally rung you from my phone. Are you having a good time?"

"I was having an amazing time until you accidentally butt-dialled me or whatever the hell you did. Now I'm cursing the fact that my name begins with an A."

"It's not what you think?"

I huffed in disbelief. "So I didn't just hear you being sucked off and shagged by your *best friend*?"

"No, well, okay, you did. But it was my last fling. You know? We get a pass don't we, on our hen and stag do's?"

"No, we most definitely do not." I told him, wishing to God I'd shagged that fittie from the club, because I might feel better right now if I had.

"What do you mean, Chris Mellon? I'm not a pass. We've been shagging on and off for years. It's time for you to make your mind up, her or me." Tania's voice yelled out.

"Tell that slag you choose me." I commanded. "Tell her you love me more than life, and she'll never measure up."

"Anna..."

"Tell her." I screamed.

"Tania. You're my best friend, but Anna... I," he cleared his throat. "I love her more than life and you'll never measure up."

There was a banshee style scream and a yell of "My eye, my eye." Then a door slammed.

"She's gone. I'm sorry, Anna. It meant nothing. I can't wait for our wedding."

"I'm not marrying you, you fucking cheating bastard. Make sure all your belongings are out of our house for when I get back home. You hear me? Or I'll tell my dad and he'll throw you the fuck out."

"Anna. Please? We need to talk. Don't be hasty."

"Chris, you're a dickhead." I screeched, just as Lesley and Susan came through the door of the hotel room.

Lesley turned to Susan. "Told you."

CHAPTER Three

In Dublin's Fare City

Anna

Beeeeepp, beeeeep, beeeepp, beeeep.

"Can they shut the fuck up?" Susan shouted towards the window. "Don't they know we've someone needs a bit of peace and quiet?"

The taxis had been beeping non-stop for hours now, dropping off and picking up fares at the rank directly opposite our hotel room. It was annoying as all hell because the alcohol I'd consumed added to the shock of the phone call had made me sleepy. If they could just stop with the noise, I'd be able to shut my eyes and pretend none of this had happened.

Instead, we had the light on while everyone kept watching me like I was a suicide risk even though I was now in my fluffy pyjamas. It was gone four am and in all honesty I wanted to be on my own, but that wasn't possible due to my sharing a room with three other women.

"I know it doesn't seem like it now, love, but it will be the best thing in the long run." Lesley said, smothering me in an embrace where I was almost suffocated by her 38E chest. Men would have died to be in my position but I quite liked breathing.

My bottom lip wobbled. "Lesley, Chris has been cheating on me. How could he do that? I thought he loved me?"

"Oh, love, I think he loved you - loves you - just he loves himself more. And that Tania... I never trusted her. She was always giving you the evil eye when you weren't looking."

"Wh-why didn't you tell me?"

"I've told you the whole way through that the bloke was a dickhead, but I didn't know he was up to anything. I just thought he was in love with himself."

"Do you think he's done it before? I wonder how long he's been sleeping with Tania?"

"That's a conversation you need to have with him." Jenny said. "I'm going to ring Kian in the morning and see if he knows anything, and if he's been covering for him, there will be hell to pay in our house."

I shook my head. "No, Jen. Don't let it cause trouble for you two. If Chris has been messing around, it's not Kian's fault and it would put him in an awkward position. Even if he knows, let him be. This is on Chris, and like you say, I need to talk to him about things. Huh, and I thought Ireland was a place of luck."

"Sorry, lovely." Lesley patted my arm this time, thank goodness. "Let's try to get some sleep now, okay? If these GODDAMN TAXIS EVER STOP BEEPING. Then tomorrow we can just have an easy day. We'll do a bit of the tourist thing, try to take your mind off stuff before you go home."

They turned the lights off. I was sharing a bed with Jenny. There was a lot of tossing and turning but eventually everyone settled and I could tell by the change in their breathing that tiredness had won over the noise from outside.

I turned my head and let tears run from my face down into my pillow.

My fiance had cheated on me. Now I had another day in Dublin with the girls on what should have been a weekend of laughter. Instead it would no doubt drag like a slow motion dental appointment for an extraction. Shopping was not going to cheer me up. Every time I closed my eyes I couldn't help but put images to the voices that had come out of my phone speakers. My fiance's cock in another woman's mouth and pussy.

There was no way back from that. I knew it. No matter how much he begged, it was over.

Six years down the toilet because he'd shit where he ate.

We went down to breakfast via the hotel reception where Susan complained about our room. I wouldn't have wanted to be the receptionist dealing with her. She came back and I swear steam was about to come out of her ears.

"They won't change the room. Said they are the rooms allocated to our discount provider, and we'd need to take it up with them. She said no one usually complains, but the taxis do it because other drivers fall asleep at the wheel while they're waiting."

"No one usually complains? Does the company booking their rooms usually run trips for deaf people?" Lesley looked ready to lamp somebody.

My shoulders slumped. "I'm sorry, ladies. This trip has turned into a complete bag of shit. When I've saved up I'll pay you all back, okay?"

"Don't be silly." Jenny said and all three of them gathered around me.

"We had a great time last night, didn't we? Until we found out about Chris?"

I nodded.

"And we have all of today. So are we going to let this spoil things? Well, yes, it will a bit, but there's nothing to stop us eating lovely food, checking out the shops and doing a spot of sightseeing is there? So, come on. Let's get breakfast, showered and then hit the sights."

I wished I had half as much enthusiasm as Jenny. I wasn't stupid and knew this was to try to gee me up and make the most of the rest of our break. So I vowed to do it - for them. I would hold myself together for the day and then once I was home tomorrow I would deal with whatever I needed to do to get Chris out of my life. Then I'd lock myself in my house and dissolve.

"I'm ready for some toast to soak up some of the night's booze. Anyone else?" I said and set off towards the breakfast room.

The day dragged on, and I did my best to hold it together. I'm sure the others knew I was putting a brave face on things, but I didn't blame them for going along with me. We fake enjoyed wandering around Temple Bar and other busy areas, until eventually we reached the statue of Molly Malone, something I'd actually heard of.

"They say it's good luck to rub her tits." Lesley cackled.

"Well I've nothing to lose." I said walking over and copping a good feel of Molly's boobs. The other three followed suit and then we heard a sing-song start up. There was a group of people in front of the statue, all linking arms, being led by a guy with brown hair, whose head I could just see the top of over the statue. His Irish lilt encouraged them to join in.

"Aww, come on, let's go join in." Lesley began dragging my reluctant body over. I guessed she was trying to inject a bit of lighthearted fun into proceedings and I was fine... at first. Then it all went wrong.

CHAPTER Four

The end of Molly Malone

Cillian

Just my feckin luck. Out with the lads and I see the woman of my dreams. Seriously, my friends thought it was the beer talking but I honest to God, saw that blonde-haired beauty in that skintight green glittery dress and I thought, I'm gonna marry that girl.

Trouble was when I made a move, she was already getting married.

Whoever he was I wanted to murder him with my bare hands.

And then, she kissed me. Talk about rubbing salt in the wound.

That kiss had been electric and spoke straight to my cock. I thought I might be in for a one night stand with Mrs I'm-marrying-someone-who-isn't-you, but then she ran off to be sick.

I made her sick.

After that I'd gone home. I was working the next day anyway, so I figured I might as well get my head down and forget about her. It'll have been the drink messing with my brain like my mates said.

I worked as a tour guide around Dublin, giving talks on the history of the place. I ran a daytime walking tour and an evening ghost one. It was good craic. I liked talking to people and meeting visitors from all over the world, and I'd like to think I brought a bit of entertainment to the mix.

So Sunday afternoon I pulled my group of twenty in front of the statue of Molly Malone and told my rapt audience the story about the mystery surrounding whether Molly actually ever existed.

"So who knows the song then? Shall we have ourselves a little sing-song? I'll start." I coughed ready to sing my heart out.

"In Dublin's fair city, where the girls are so-"

I stopped for a second though thankfully my crowd carried on regardless.

But she was there, at the end of the row. The woman of my dreams. Well, I think it was her. Her eyes were puffy, and she looked miserable. No doubt the result of the hangover she'd woken up with this morning.

Her and three friends joined in the sing-song, so I made sure to make it my best effort. But my mystery girl never looked up at me once. Her face kept to the floor, and she didn't join in until we got to the part where Molly died and then she sang loudly and mournfully, and... like a strangled cat. The rest of the crowd looked at her but she didn't notice and as we got to the end, she started to cry and a friend put an arm around her and led her away.

"And that concludes the tour. Thank you ladies and gentlemen." I informed them as I dashed off, missing my opportunity for tips. I touched one of her friends on the back. She stopped and turned to me, a crease to her brow.

"She alright, your friend there? Only I met her last night at the club."

The woman, with mid-length brown hair, looked me up and down so hard I'd swear I'd forgotten to get dressed.

"She will be. She doesn't know it yet, but the best thing just happened to her."

"Oh yeah?"

"You're very interested for someone who just met her last night." She raised an eyebrow.

"Yeah, I am. She seemed lovely, though drunk, and now she looks upset. No-one should come to

Dublin and be upset. I've just finished work so is there anything I can do?"

"You could fly over to Sheffield and kick the ever loving shit out of her cheating fiance. That'd be a start."

"What?"

She tapped my arm and looked over her shoulder where her friends were almost out of view. "Listen, I need to go. Looks like the idiots don't even realise I'm not with them. Anna's had her heart broken, so it's a waste of time you being interested in her. Thanks for asking, but she's got her friends and we're flying back home in the morning."

"What's her surname? Is she on Facebook?" I was desperate by now not to let her walk out of my life a second time.

The woman sighed but smiled. "Persistent aren't you? She's Anna Hepplestone, from Hackenthorpe. She's on Facebook, but for God's sake give her time to come to terms with what just happened to her, okay? Right, I've got to go."

I looked and her friends were beckoning to her.

"Thank you. Safe journey back okay? Her ex is obviously a fecking eejit and I might just fly over and kick the ever loving shit out of him yet."

The woman laughed. "I like you. My name's Lesley. I gotta go. What's your name?"

"Cillian. Cillian McCarthy."

"Well bye, Cillian. It was nice to meet you. Sorry

for gatecrashing your sing-a-long. We hadn't noticed it was a tour."

With that she sped up to catch up to her friends and once more my new found crush left me standing.

But now I had a name.

Anna Hepplestone.

I found her immediately on Facebook. Her smiling face gazing out on her profile picture. Maybe I should give her time before sending her a friend request? Then I thought about her lowlife fiance. What if she took him back, and I lost her again?

I'd send it now. Feck it.

CHAPTER Five

Out with the old

Anna

They insisted on us going back to the hotel in a taxi. Susan sat up front with the driver and proceeded to lecture him about all the beeping outside the hotel room. Did she think it would actually stop them? I'd just decided fuck it, whatever would be, would be. I could catch up on however much sleep I liked when I got home, as long as I worked it around my shifts at the Nag's Head, and I could always take more annual leave if it all got too much.

We got to the room, and I threw myself on my bed, a fresh batch of tears streaming down my face.

"I'm sorry. I was trying not to let it get to me."

"Don't be silly." said Susan. "I took ages to process my divorce, and I was the one who instigated it. We don't expect you to be okay a few hours later. We were just trying to make the best of the trip. Lesley looked to see if there was an earlier flight home, but there wasn't anything."

"You're such good friends." I told them. "I'm dreading going home and having to face him. Then what will people be saying? I'll be the talk of the pub. 'That's her, that's the one got cheated on and had to cancel the wedding'."

"Better that than be finding out after the wedding, like when you could have had a baby or something."

I nodded. "Yeah, glad I found out now. Though I'm not sure babies were on the agenda. Chris wasn't keen. I was hoping to talk him around after the wedding, but now I'm wondering just how much of his behaviour I've allowed him to get away with over the years."

"Look, I think we should have a relax here for a while." Lesley patted my leg. "I could pop and get us a few buns and a bottle of wine. Then we can see if you feel like going out for a meal later for our last evening. No pressure."

"Thanks, Lesley. That sounds good. I'm going to check Facebook to see if the gossip has hit yet."

I opened up Facebook and looked at my profile. There was nothing. Just general notifications about people I didn't really give a shit about. I had a friend request and clicked on it. Some guy called Cillian

McCarthy. No friends in common. Profile picture of a guy with a beer glass in front of his face. Couldn't make much out with it being so small. Probably a pervert who would send me a dick pic if I accepted.

"Anything?" Lesley asked.

"Nah. Just a friend request from a pervert. No friends in common so I'll-"

The phone was snatched out of my hand and Lesley flicked through. "Cillian McCarthy. Friend request accepted." She sounded like the recorded voice on my answering machine at home.

My eyes went wide. "What are you doing? Pass me my phone back, you lunatic."

"I know who he is. I met him earlier. He was the bloke singing near the statue."

I rubbed my forehead. "So how's he got my Facebook details? Are you trying to set me up? I only got jilted yesterday for fuck's sake."

She shook her head from side to side and sighed. "No. Calm yourself down. He spoke to me after the singing. Said he met you in the club the night before. So I gave him your details."

"Give me my phone. I want to click on his profile. I could have spoken to anyone that night."

She passed it back to me slowly. I snatched it and pressed on his profile and then onto photos.

It was him.

The one I clearly remembered kissing.

Most of that night prior to Chris' accidental

phone call might have been a blank, but my body had remembered the kiss. And he wanted to be my Facebook friend. Why?

The deed was done. He was accepted. I wouldn't be doing anything further from my side of things. I had enough man trouble as it was. However, the fact he was now one of my Facebook friends, tenuously connected to me, gave me a strange thrill.

"You can make this up to me by fetching that wine."

We drank wine, and we did pop out for a meal. Then we came back, packed our stuff and chatted until the early hours where we tried and failed to fall asleep amongst the cacophony of the beeping horns and revellers' shouts.

The next morning we all went down for breakfast and then it was time to make our way back to the airport to catch the plane to Manchester followed by a train back to Sheffield. Then I'd have to face the music, or bellend as I now referred to my ex. I switched my phone off aeroplane mode when we got to Manchester to see five messages from him. Drunk texts with apologies and him begging for forgiveness. I deleted them all and as the notifications moved up my screen, I saw I had a Facebook message from Cillian McCarthy.

I pressed open.

Your friend told me what happened. Don't forgive a guy who could cheat on you. You are worth more. I know that, and I only met you for a few minutes before you ran off to throw up.

Don't worry, I won't message again. I'm sure you have enough to deal with right now. But I'm here and a new friend if you need one. Someone who can be a shoulder to cry on if required, albeit from Dublin.

It was a pleasure to meet you.

C.

"What are you smiling at? Bloody hell, it's nice to see one of those on your face, lass." Lesley tried to look at my phone. "I'm just glad I'm going home, that's all, even if it is to face the bellend. I want my own bed and a night of quiet - no car horns allowed. Now let's get that train and get home."

As the cab pulled up outside my house, the curtains

twitched. I should have known he'd be there waiting for me. I'd bet my month's salary that he'd not moved a single thing out of our home, thinking he could talk me around. The more I thought about it, there had been various suspicious behaviours over the years and I'd always believed his excuses. I moved as fast as I could to the front door as it was pissing it down with rain and hoped dickhead didn't think I was rushing to see him. Now as I saw his sheepish face in the doorway as he let me into the house, it was like the blinkers had fallen off and I saw my ex-fiance in all his lying glory.

"Anna. I can explain."

I stood in the hallway, coat on and luggage at my feet. "Do you think you could give me a fucking chance to get in the house? This shows what a selfish bastard you are. I'm not even through the door. You could have taken my case and helped a bit, but no, you just stand there like the knob you are trying to talk me around. I'm going upstairs to change and unpack and I'll talk to you when I'm good and fucking ready. Now make yourself useful and put the kettle on. I'm dying for a cuppa."

"Oh, of course, darlin'. You're right. I'm just so desperate to sort things out between us, but yes, you go get unpacked and settled. I'll make you a drink and then when you're ready, we can talk."

As I unpacked my belongings, he walked in with a hot cuppa. He placed it on the top of the chest of drawers at the side of me and had the audacity to lean over to kiss me. I moved my face away.

"I missed you while you were gone." He said.

I waited until he'd left the room and that was it. The straw that broke the camels back. He'd missed me? At which point? When his cock was in Tania's hoo-ha had he missed the warmth of mine?

Unfastening the front window and pushing it wide open I went to Chris' wardrobe and gathered armfuls of clothing. Then I threw his clothes outside, watching them land on the soggy front lawn. I thanked God for the despicable weather. With every single clothing item of his gone from the room, including his pants and socks, I stormed downstairs with my empty cup in my hand.

As he came towards me and opened his mouth, I threw it at him. It hit him in the forehead before bouncing onto the carpet, thankfully unbroken as it was a favourite cup. Plus, now it had caused him an injury I loved it even more. He clutched his forehead and followed me into the kitchen where I reached into my odds and sods drawer and took out a roll of black sacks.

"Your clothes are all in the front garden. Hopefully they've blown away or someone's stolen them, but you might want to bag them up otherwise and put them in your car. If they're brought back in here, I'm having a bonfire."

"Anna, be reasonable."

I stood, hands on hips, and narrowed my gaze on him.

"Be reasonable? Let's hear it then. What's your excuse for what happened?"

He bowed his head in his 'shame' pose and looked up through his pale blonde fringe. "Babe, I should have known, but Tania's had a crush on me for ages. I'm a bloke though. I genuinely thought she was just a mate. Don't forget as well that I was pissed cos it was my stag do. Don't remember much, just waking up and thinking me and you were doing it. Then I saw it was Tania, and I chucked her off me and out of the house. Told her I never wanted to see her again."

My mouth dropped open, and I held out both my hands palms up. "Are you for fucking real? I heard it all. You butt-dialled me. My God, you can't even say it was a mistake and you're sorry. You're blaming Tania. Do you know what, Chris? I don't blame Tania. She's single. You weren't. No matter how much she came onto you, you still had a choice to say no. But you didn't. You shagged her, and then I heard you bin her off like she was a piece of shit. Well, darlin'" I said the word as sarcastically as I could muster. "I hope she realises she can do better than you. I know I can. Now get the fuck out of my house, and if you don't I'm ringing my dad."

Chris' face paled. My dad was an ex-bouncer, who now worked as a bailiff. "You're making a mistake ending us. Six years down the pan. You won't ever find another me, you know."

"Thank fuck for that." I yelled, and I threw the thick roll of bin liners at him, scoring another direct hit, this time right in his filthy mouth.

When he'd gone, I looked around and realised that I needed a do-over. I needed to clean this house within an inch of its life. I had no idea where the energy came from but I cleaned that house with bleach and other cleaning products from top-to-bottom, throwing anything of Chris' into the spare room for him to collect some other time. Then I dragged off all the bedding and threw that and the mattress into the back garden. It was time for a bonfire. I'd order a new mattress this afternoon. For now, I'd sleep on the sofa. I doubted I'd get much sleep tonight anyway.

Thoroughly exhausted, I flopped onto said sofa where it all hit me at once: exhaustion, sorrow, anger. I spent the rest of the day and evening going between crying my eyes out, throwing things, and dozing. I answered concerned texts from my friends. Jenny said Kian didn't agree with cheats and he'd vowed never to see Chris again. Apparently Chris had borrowed money off him several times and not paid him back so he was glad to be 'shut of the sponger'. She said he'd only stayed mates with him because of our friendship.

Lesley sent a text and said she was ready to meet me if I wanted to get drunk.

I lay on the sofa and stared at the ceiling, wondering how I would tell my family and how devastating it would be cancelling everything and losing all those deposits. How had my life crashed and burned so damn fast?

CHAPTER Six

Deja Foo

Anna

Bless them. Jenny and Kian, then Lesley and Susan, had come in on my evening shift the following day to make sure the first one post-breakup went okay. Dan, the pub landlord and my boss, had been extra fussy, telling me I could go out back if needed. He'd had a traumatic divorce, so he knew how devastating the ending of a relationship was.

I felt loved and supported. In fact, all was well. Yes, my eyes were a little red and puffy and had required extra make-up for me to look half-human. I blamed a cold to any customers who enquired. My new mattress had arrived, I'd nipped to the local supermarket for some bedding, and every trace of Chris was shut away in the spare room. I was rid.

Well, I was until he walked in, holding hands with Tania.

"The brass fucking cheek of him." Rachel yelled. "Shall I refuse to serve him, Dan?"

Dan shook his head. "You can't. He's a patron. I know what he did to Anna was wrong, but he's not stepped out of line here... yet." Dan said ominously. "Do you want to go out back?" He asked me.

I shook my head and stood up straight. "No. I'm not moving. This is where I work." I approached them. "What can I get you?" I turned to Tania. "Would you like my liver or a kidney next, seeing as you seem to be taking my things?"

She pulled Chris closer to her. "I'm sorry, Anna. That's why I wanted to come in. I love him. I always have. And he loves me. We tried to resist but our love is too strong."

"You do realise that yesterday he was begging me to take him back, right?"

You could have heard a customer take a drink of their pint, the pub had gone that quiet, as they took in the evening's entertainment.

"Oh Anna. I know that's not true, and it was the other way around. We've come to show you that you need to accept the situation. We're together now, and well, we're getting married."

My jaw dropped open.

"If it's okay with you, we'll buy you out of everything arranged so far. My mum and dad have a wedding fund for me so it's no problem, and we'll get married when you would have."

I tilted my head nearer towards her as I was sure I was hearing things. "You want my wedding?"

"Yes, well everything apart from the dress. I'm only a size eight."

There were audible gasps from some of the customers.

"Yes. Agreed." I said, reaching over and shaking her hand. I'd be rid and my parents would have their money back. I'd only be down the price of a dress and I could sell that locally. If she wanted to embarrass herself having my wedding and hitch herself to the loser standing in front of me she could have at it.

I tapped a finger across my lips. "Oh, actually. I have one condition to our agreement."

"Oh, what's that?" She replied. I noted that Chris had stood at her side like the dummy he was and had yet to speak.

"You never step a foot in this pub again, either of you. Because if you do, I will lose my job."

Tania's brow creased. "I don't follow."

"I'll punch your lights out if you come in again. Now fuck off." I told them.

Tania knew when she was shit out of luck.

"Come on, Chris. Let's go."

I watched as he followed her out of the pub like a dog following its master.

Lesley applauded and the rest of the pub followed suit. I must have gone beet red as my face felt like it would combust with the heat. "Atta girl. You did so well there."

"You really did." Rachel added. "You are so fucking better off without that knobhead. God, how can she just step into another woman's wedding like that? All that's different is the pussy. It's a case of deja foo."

I nodded and tried to smile, but I was struggling to hold it together as the reality hit that my wedding really was off, my relationship over, and my fiance was about to marry someone else.

"Do you know, I think I will go work out back for a bit." I told Dan.

As expected my parents hit the roof, with my dad threatening to kneecap Chris. Once they'd calmed down, I asked my mum to liaise with Chris' to get everything transferred and our money back. My mum talked to the woman at the dress agency and it was agreed that we would just lose the deposit as it was a popular style and she felt it would resell easily.

With everything finally finished and Chris completely removed from my life, I threw myself into painting and decorating my home the way I wanted it to look, and working. I found evenings at home unusually quiet though. Lesley kept asking me to meet her for drinks but I wasn't a big social creature and I wanted to get used to my own space.

Which is how I found myself one night having drunk the best part of a bottle of wine on my own, lying feet up on the sofa, with two cushions behind my back, my laptop on my knees and Facebook open.

I clicked into Cillian's page to see what he'd been up to. Something I'd been doing ever since I got home. He updated it rarely and there was nothing new there.

I opened his message and re-read it. Then I thought fuck it and started typing my own.

Hi Cillian.

What have you been up to lately? I cancelled my wedding and have been redecorating my home.

I wish my trip to Dublin had been more enjoyable, but I still remember your friendly face.

Thanks for the friend request and sorry it's taken me so long to respond.

Sod it.
SEND.

I put my laptop on the floor and enjoyed the last of the bottle of wine before settling back on the sofa and closing my eyes. When I woke a while later, drool running down the side of my mouth, I decided it was time to make my way up to bed. As I lifted the laptop off the floor to close it down, I saw I'd had a reply.

Anna!

So good to hear from you.

Sorry about what happened to you.
How are you feeling?
Glad you remember my 'friendly face'.
Do you remember anything else ;)

Oh fuck. I thought. Perhaps I'd better re-read the message in the morning when I was more sober and more awake. I closed the laptop and went to bed.

CHAPTER Seven

The morning after

Cillian

I couldn't believe she messaged me back! I'd honestly thought me cyber stalking her was as far as it would ever go and to be honest her Facebook page was the most boring page ever. All she did was talk about books, of which she'd read loads since she ended it with that shitehawk. I worried a bit when I sent my message back that night and there was no reply, but I needn't have. It was the start of a series of long messages with the woman of my dreams (and fantasies, but let's not go there right now).

Anna: Hope you don't mind me messaging you again. I must apologise, I only ever seem to converse with you when I'm blad-

dered. Yes, I do remember that night and now I'm sober and blushing!

Cillian: Don't blush. Anyway, how are you? Do you fancy having an Irish Facebook pen-friend?

Anna: Sounds good. I'm okay. Do you know my ex-fiance bought me out of my half of the wedding and is now marrying his female best friend on our wedding day? I'm well rid of that one.

Cillian: Are you fecking kidding me? Shall I get on a plane and come kill him for you?

Anna: No. I'm glad he's out of my life. I've rediscovered my love of books.

Cillian: I'd noticed. All your posts are about them!

Anna: Well Chris, my ex, used to talk all the time when I was trying to read. It's nice to have the peace, and it's good to escape into fictional worlds if I'm finding things a bit tough.

Cillian: Understandable. So tell me more about yourself. Family. Where you work, etc. Fave colour lol.

Anna: Okay. 28-year-old jilted bride. I work behind the bar at a local pub. Rent a house which I've been decorating to my own taste. Love reading, like to switch up between thrillers and romantic comedies. At the moment reading lots of books where people are brutally murdered, can't think why ;)

My dad is a Bailiff, my mum a secretary, and I have an older brother and sister who are both married with their own families. My favourite colour is … *drum roll* … red!

Your turn!

Cillian: 29-year-old lazy fecker. Still live with my parents. My ma says she wants me to get settled down and feck off as soon as possible, like yesterday. I'm a tour guide. I don't read. I do like listening to music, mainly rock. Keen photographer and often take myself off around Dublin to snap the main sights and the less well known ones.

My ma is a housewife, my da works in I.T. I also have two older siblings. Mine are both sisters, again with their own families. They babied me and that's why I've probably not completely grown up yet.

I don't have a favourite colour, that's girly shite!

Anna: It is not girly to have a favourite colour. I bet if I looked in your wardrobe I'd discover you had a preference for one over another!
Also I think you should challenge yourself and get your own place. Just think, you could display your photographs and play your music to your hearts content!

Cillian: Gah you sound like my ma. Is she paying you?

Anna: pahahahaha.

Funnily enough though Anna got me thinking. Because maybe I did need to get my own place and stand on my own two feet? Let my parents enjoy some time without me being in the way. Plus, what if Anna ever wanted to visit? I mean she probably wouldn't; we were just mates. But if she did?

I decided I'd look for a place just in case, and maybe one day, I'd ask her if she wanted to come see it! Heading to the kitchen to get a bite to eat, I caught sight of myself in the mirror. God, you're a tool Cillian, moping for a lass you had one snog with who lives miles away. Ah well, if nothing ever happened at least I had somewhere I could crash out shitfaced without my mother moaning on that I made the house stink of ale and woke her up.

May 2018

Cillian: I did it, Anna. I'm all moved in. If I'm short of rent one month, can you help me out as this independence is all your fault.

Anna: No. Just drink less on a weekend.

Cillian: Thanks for the moving in present. I've always wanted a set of bright red tea towels.

Anna: I hope to God you spotted the gift card inside, and it's to be spent wisely. Not ordering a bottle of whiskey. The red can remind you of me when you're doing the dishes.

Cillian: Doing the dishes? You mean throwing takeout cartons in the bin? Plus, ooops on the whiskey, hic!

Anna: How's your ma taking it now?

Cillian: She's stopped crying that her baby has left. All that fuss after she kept going on about me leaving. Now she's decorating the spare room and making it an 'artist's studio'. My da winked at me and thanked me for moving out. He's looking forward to some peace and quiet on the times their grandbabies aren't around. No peace and quiet when that lot descends.

So anyway bossy boots. I moved out. My turn to set you a challenge. You've to go do something social one night a week other than go down the pub for work. You need to start embracing life again. So knitting class, yoga. What's it to be?

Anna: Hmmm, I'll have a look around and a think. You mean I actually have to put my book down and leave the house? *sigh*

June 2018

Anna: My photography teacher says I have a natural talent. I reckon I can probably take better photos than you.

Cillian: You know when I suggested a class, I didn't mean steal my hobby and make me look shite at it.

Anna: *shrugs*

Cillian: Cheeky mare. Show us some of these photos then.
Cillian: Bloody hell. They really are good, Anna. Have you thought of studying this professionally?

Anna: Well, I've seen your photos and they're just as good so have YOU thought of studying it professionally?

Cillian: Maybe, sometimes. Bit pie in the sky though isn't it? I can hear my da in my ear telling me to get a proper job.

Anna: And by that did he mean work as a tour guide?

Cillian: Well…

Anna: I challenge you to look into studying photography as a potential career. I'm not just yet because I'm enjoying my starter course and that's just looking slightly too far ahead. However, I will do in the future if I continue to enjoy it. Deal?

Cillian: Deal.

Anna: You alive? Not heard from you in a couple of days?

Cillian: Sorry, had a sickness bug. Did find

a course though. Starts in September and I could work my tour guiding around it.

Anna: That's brilliant. Tell me more.

*Cillian: *barf emoticon**

Anna: Oh okay, I'll message you tomorrow to see if you're feeling better.

Cillian: :D

July 2018

Cillian: So what shall I challenge you to do this month?

Anna: Get through what should have been my wedding day?

Cillian: Oh shite. Is that today?

Anna: No. It's in two weeks. Saturday 14 July. I'm staring at the calendar where I'd

forgotten I'd put a heart around the date. Everyone in the pub will be staring at me. My friends will be suffocating. I'm dreading it, Cillian. Tell me what to do. Set me a challenge.

Cillian: Okay, here it is. Come back to Dublin. You can stay in my spare room. Come and let me show you Dublin as it should be seen and get away from that place until it's all over. Stop a week. You have annual leave, don't you?

Anna: *Shocked face emoticon* I can't do that, that's insane.

Cillian: Why is it? Is it because I'm male? If a female friend asked you to get away from it, you'd do it, wouldn't you? Well, I'm a friend. Book into a hotel if you feel better. Redo Dublin and discover its magic. You were shortchanged last time. What have you got to lose? This is my challenge; push yourself - and bring your camera.

She didn't reply and for the next thirty minutes as I sat there waiting for a response I thought I'd gone too far. I thought I'd lost her and the next thing would be an unfriending. A cutting off of contact. But then the message appeared.

Anna: Challenge accepted. Dan says I can have leave. Does Thursday 12 July sound okay for me arriving and thanks for the offer of a room, but I'm going to book a hotel. You, however, can be my own personal tour guide.

Cillian: That sounds grand and it will be my pleasure.

My heart thudded in my chest. She was coming back to Dublin. The best kisser I'd ever met, the girl of my dreams, was on her way back to Dublin in ten days time.

She might come back to my flat. I looked around at the empty takeaway cartons, crushed cans of beer, and general manky surroundings. God. I would have to up my game.

I rang my ma.

"Ma, it's me. Could you teach me how to cook something?"

"Pardon?"

"Could you teach me how to cook? I can do a fry up, but can you teach me how to do something traditional like your stew, and colcannon? Sometime this week."

"Stall the ball there, son."

I waited.

"Darragh?" She shouted into the background.

"Yeah?"

"Phone the hospital, I'm having a hallucination. I heard your son say he wants to learn how to cook."

"What? Pass me the phone."

I sighed. "Hi, Da."

"Don't cook for her, son. Take her out to dinner. Less mess for you to clean up and less interference from your ma. Ow. God, she's a punch on her still."

"It's me, your ma. You come over tomorrow and I'll teach you some basics. Yes, take her for dinner, but if she comes back, she'll want something to eat. Always made me hungry, did lovemaking."

"Oh my God, Ma. I'm hanging up right now." I said.

Then when I hung up, I smiled, wondering if Miss Anna Hepplestone would indeed end up in my bed. I'd imagined her there often enough.

CHAPTER Eight

The Irish Raver

Anna

I sat in Pizza Express and munched on a dough ball as I awaited my main course.

Jenny was sitting opposite me still wearing an expression like I'd told her I was having surgery to become a man.

"You've been messaging with him all these months and you didn't think to share that fact with your best mate?"

I shrugged. "I thought about it a few times, but I didn't know if you'd be all, 'Oh that's not a good idea, Anna. What if he's a serial killer, and he hunts you down?'."

"Why on earth would I have said that? Actually, what I would have said was tell me every single detail of what you've been chatting about with this guy, and also what's the back story? How did you meet? How did he get your details?"

"Okay." I had a quick drink and then put my glass down. "So no judging me, but when I was drunk, and we were in that club in Dublin, I danced with this guy. I remember him being sexy as fuck but thought it was beer goggles, and, well, I may have snogged him."

"You did, or didn't? Do you not remember?"

I sighed. "No, I did. I snogged him and my drunken mind thought it was the most fabulous kiss ever."

"And then what?"

"And then I wanted to be sick and ran off. That's when you found me in the toilets. Then we went back to the hotel. Only he was the tour guide that next day, you know where you dragged me for the sing-song? He saw me and got my details from Lesley. Sent me a message. When I was feeling bored one night, I sent one back, and that was it. We've been in touch ever since."

"You are in so much trouble for keeping this from me. I wonder if he was really a good kisser, or if it was the beer? Oooh you'll be able to find out."

I shook my head. "No, I won't. I'm just going to sightsee and meet my friend."

"Are you insane?"

I raised an eyebrow. "Now I expected you to say that about my getting on a plane and going to Dublin on my own, not about the fact I refuse to lock lips with a man I met one night when drunk."

"Well there's that too, but it sounds so romantic. Hey, what about if me and Kian came along? We could hang around in the background or something?"

"Absolutely not. I'm going alone. But I'll keep checking in with you, so you know he's not murdered me. To be honest, I'm going to spend some time on my own, not just be with Cillian all week. I'm an independent woman now. It's time to embrace it."

"Well, you could embrace the one night stand. Have a fuck of the Irish." She fell about laughing at her own joke.

"I'm going to behave myself."

"For a whole week?"

I nodded. "For the entire week."

"Even if without beer goggles he's hot as hell?"

"He is. I've seen his Facebook photos remember?"

"Show me." She demanded.

I was getting his profile on screen when my pizza arrived.

"Funghi?" The waitress asked.

"That's hers." Jenny said. "Might not be the only fun guy she's eating too."

The waitress laughed as I turned bright red. "You did not just say that."

"I did." She took the phone from me and clicked through his photos. "If you don't fuck this guy, then you're even more insane. If he is indeed a serial killer, at least you'll die with a huge smile on your face."

"We're just friends."

"Anna?"

"Mmmm hmmm." I mumbled while chewing my food.

"Just don't discount it altogether. If you get along and there's a spark, go for it. Promise me."

"I promise. But my focus is on enjoying Dublin. I've had a romance ruin the place for me once. I don't want it happening again."

"Fair enough." She said, handing me my phone back. "You're gonna make sure you shaved everywhere and pack a razor though, yeah? Or go and get a wax?"

"Is sex all you think about?"

"Well, yeah. Better than thinking about the fact the bins need emptying."

"Poor Kian. He must be knackered."

"He was pleased as punch I was coming out tonight to give him a night off."

We giggled.

Jenny's face turned serious, and she lowered her voice. "So, how are you about the whole 14 July thing?"

"Numb." I replied honestly. "I feel like it all happened to someone else. Now I can't believe what I ever saw in him. I fell out of love so fast that I'm questioning if I was ever in love. I think I was in-settling."

Jenny picked up her glass and took a sip. "Chris was always a charmer and I think when you first met him, he was an okay guy. At least he seemed to be, and that's how Kian knew him, or we'd have never set you two up. But he got cocky as he got older. Neither of us expected him to cheat on you though."

"Oh, I've heard stories since, people at the Nag's feel they need to share the rumours with me now. I don't think Tania's been the only one. I went for a sexual screening you know? How fucking humiliating, having to say my boyfriend had been cheating and could they check he'd not left me with a final gift before departure. Luckily, we'd always used condoms and everything came back okay. But that's not right, is it? To do that to someone. I'm glad he's gone. I don't feel sadness that I'm not marrying him, but I get upset thinking it should have been my wedding day. Does that make any sense?"

Jenny placed a hand over mine. "Yeah, I get it."

"It's the dream of it all. The white dress, the declarations of love, the promise of the future. But I think that's all it was anyway. The promise of it, the dream. My reality would have been living with a selfish, cheating scumbag who didn't want kids."

"You really think he didn't want any?"

"Yep. I thought he'd change his mind once we were married, but I bet he wouldn't have. Chris wants the world to revolve around him, he doesn't want to share the stage."

"I wonder if Tania knows that."

I threw my napkin down on the table. "Tania deserves whatever she gets. I hope as she's walking down that aisle, she realises that she's in someone else's shoes. That she hasn't even got the wedding of her dreams, she's got another woman's. Though being honest, it wasn't the wedding of my dreams either because I had to suit what my family wanted seeing as they were paying for a chunk of it, forced to invite relatives I hadn't seen since I was six. I'd much rather have eloped."

"Well, you make sure that on Saturday 14 July at 2pm, you're doing something spectacular instead, or even better, someone." She winked.

As the days passed I became more nervous. We still messaged each other and Cillian was sending me ideas of places we could visit, but it was becoming so real. Now we were talking about where he'd meet me and what time.

This. Was. Really. Happening.

I did book myself for an all over wax, a haircut and my roots touching up, and a mani-pedi. Just for myself you understand. To increase my self confidence. But then I added a box of condoms to my luggage and admitted to myself that I was hoping, that maybe, things would go really well and I might just get a bit of action in the sack before I came home. But I wasn't to let anything like that happen at the beginning. No way. Friends only and sightseeing.

I threw a few lacy bras and matching panties into my case.

A sexy little black dress.

My God if I got searched at the airport they would think I was a right little raver.

The night before I was due to travel we'd been messaging when it came up that Cillian was video calling me. I hit answer and his image popped up on screen. Fuck he was still hot, and I had no beer goggles this time.

"Oh feck. Sorry, I hit t'wrong button. Now ya having to see me ugly face. Should get a warning before t'at happens."

I continued to stare.

"Anna?"

"Oh sorry. Oh it's fine. At least tomorrow I won't vomit at the sight of you, I'll be prepared."

"Yeah, not like last time. Doesn't do a lot to a man's ego you know, when a lass runs off to be sick."

"You know full well that was all the alcohol I'd consumed and not you."

He laughed. "Well, I'll see you tomorrow, Miss Anna Hepplestone."

"See you tomorrow, Mr Cillian McCarthy."

It took me a moment longer than it needed to, to end the video call.

My God, he was gorgeous. Stare-with-my-tongue-hung-out gorgeous. How was I going to act normal around him?

The morning of travel beckoned. I got up feeling like I would hurl and after searching around the kitchen cupboards, I found a bottle of unopened whiskey, something I loved and had been introduced to by my dad. I drank some straight from the bottle, and after almost burning out my oesophagus, I poured some into a glass and added the tiniest splash of water to it, then took another mouthful. I felt much better thirty minutes later when that and a second glass had gone. It was only 9:30 am though. Once more I repacked my case and went through my mental list of what I did/used every day to make sure I had everything.

My phoned beeped and I went on to see a text from Jenny.

Jenny: Remember! The Fuck of the Irish.

I shook my head even though she couldn't see me

and I couldn't help but smile. Hers wasn't the only message. I'd gotten one from Lesley last night wishing me safe travels and advising me to try as many bars as possible.

I was getting the train straight to Manchester airport and then the 2:00pm flight out of there, arriving in Dublin just after 3:00pm. I didn't want Cillian meeting me there, so I'd put him off. I'd booked The Fleet Hotel, as Temple Bar looked a good place to reside for the week, with lots of restaurants and shops nearby. When I arrived, I just wanted to get settled in and freshen up. No way was he seeing me straight off a flight. We'd arranged to meet in the Hard Rock Cafe - which was apparently a few doors down from my hotel - at 6:30 pm, to get a bite to eat. After that he said he'd let me get an early night. We were going to fit in sightseeing around his tour guide shifts. He'd said I could either accompany him on the tours or go 'girly shopping' as he called it, because 'no way was he sitting in shops while I tried on fourteen pairs of identical looking jeans'. I'd berated him for his stereotypical nonsense and then he'd told me that his ma used to drag him round while she took his sisters shopping. Then I felt sorry as I imagined this small boy, sat bored in a shop somewhere.

A taxi beeped outside, ready to take me to the train station and then that was it. I locked the door behind me and wheeled my case down to the taxi.

I was on my way.

The flight was straightforward, and I arrived in Dublin to a pleasant day with a hint of sunshine. I decided to brave the bus as I knew it stopped near my hotel. My room was beautiful. Pale walls, soft bedding and a soft brown carpet. Almost directly opposite was a Tesco Metro so I knew I had a place nearby for snacks and magazines. Cillian had given me his mobile number and I'd had to text him on each leg of my journey. Him, and Jenny, Lesley, and my mum, who was convinced she was getting me back in pieces in separate bin liners.

I sent everyone a text to say I'd arrived safely, saying to everyone but Cillian that I'd text again later. Then swallowing down the lump in my throat, I went in the shower again, before getting my make-up on. I dressed in a pair of blue skinny jeans; and a baggy, emerald-green tee that fell off one shoulder revealing a hint of black bra strap. After pulling my hair back in a pony tail and slipping on some wedge sandals that was it. A final squirt of my travel-sized Si perfume and off out the door I went.

"Oh my God. You made me jump a foot." I squealed, as Cillian almost walked into me, a bunch of flowers in his hand.

"I was just about to knock. Only I was early, so I thought I'd escort you to the restaurant."

Recovering but nervous, I looked up at him, taking in that scruff on his chin and those beautiful hazel eyes. His facial expression turned from one of apprehension to one of lust. I recognised it because I was feeling it myself.

"Feck it." He said, and he leaned into me, placing a hand on the back of my head. His mouth came down to mine, brushing against my lips softly and then as my own opened eagerly it changed to a lip crushing kiss that almost had my knees bowing.

I'd underestimated his kiss. He was the best kisser I reckoned in the whole universe. Beer goggles had dumbed it down.

He broke off. "Dinner then?" He smiled.

I looked back at my room. "Do you fancy a coffee first?" I winked.

You brazen hussy. My brain yelled. *What about waiting? What about sightseeing?*

My libido shouted louder.

Get in there. Whooooo hoooo.

Cillian picked me up and carried me into the room, dropping the flowers onto the floor. Then he kicked the door firmly closed behind him.

Dinner could wait.

CHAPTER Nine

Room Serviced

Anna

My clothes came off a lot faster than they went on and we fell back onto my bed, barely breaking off from kissing except to move pieces of clothing between ourselves.

I was lying on my side, Cillian's legs tangled with my own, and we kissed on and on while he stroked his fingers up and down my back. Pushing me back against the bed slightly he ran a hand over the cup of my bra and edged inside, taking in the feel of my flesh before teasing my nipple to a hardened peak with his fingertips.

My breathing became laboured, more so as he pushed the bra strap down off my shoulder, exposing my breast and lowering his head down to suck my nipple into his mouth.

"Ohhhh."

The fingers of his right hand trailed down my side and while his mouth was busy, his fingers crept under the material of my panties and began teasing my clit, before entering my heat and then returning to tease me again. I bet this guy could rub his stomach in a circle while patting his head at the same time, and I made a note to ask him before my brain turned on me and yelled.

Are you fucking stupid? You're getting laid. Concentrate.

I'd had a couple of lovers before Chris, but I'd been with him all those years and while he was good in bed, I'd kind of got used to the order of proceedings and a lot of the time I'd have to admit to faking it to get it over with. It came to me then, while I had another man's mouth and fingers on me, that I'd got bored and been more interested in the wedding than in the guy I was actually marrying.

Then Cillian pushed me back onto the bed, pulled down my panties and placed his mouth over my clit and all my thoughts aside from 'Oh my God' disappeared.

His tongue darted and teased. He lifted his head up.

"Open your eyes." He said in that beautiful accent.

My no doubt lust-fuelled gaze focused on him.

"You're beautiful and I'd rather feast on you than

that restaurant food any day of the week." He smirked and then returned his attentions to my core.

My stomach answered for me by letting out an enormous rumble, causing Cillian to shake with laughter while he dined on me. His tongue plunged inside me and I bucked up off the bed, my head back against the pillow, my breasts arching outwards.

"Oh my God. I'm so close."

He picked up speed, and I clutched at his head with my hands as I came over his face, rocked by tremors.

Breathless, I collapsed back against the bed, lifting an arm and part covering my face with my hand.

He climbed back up the bed and lying next to me he moved my hand and stared into my face.

"It's no good going shy now."

I blushed. "Thank you, that was, well, amazing."

He turned onto his back. "My pleasure."

I couldn't help but notice his rather large erection tenting his boxer briefs and thought the least I could do was stroke it and see where we ended up. I moved in closer and let my fingers trail down his abdomen and down the waistband of his boxers.

He turned and caught my lips with his own again as I fastened my hand around his shaft and began to stroke his velvety soft cock. He let out a satisfied sigh.

My hand was restricted within the confines of

the boxers so I broke off from our kissing and sat up, getting hold of the waistband. Cillian raised his hips as I pulled his boxers down and discarded them to the floor. His dick looked a decent size, certainly an inch larger than I was used to. It was purple and angry looking, like it was straining for release. Fastening my hand back around him I lowered my head and captured him in my mouth.

"Ahhh."

I stroked the base of his shaft while my tongue swirled around his tip and then I sucked on him, taking him as far back in my throat as I could. I increased my speed, but Cillian stopped me.

"Oh no, sweetheart. I'm not coming in your mouth tonight. Not first anyway. I want inside you."

"Do you have a condom?" I asked him. "Because I have some if not."

A cheeky grin broke out over his face. "Did you anticipate this happening, or did you just bring them in case any bloke in Dublin fancied throwing it into ya?"

I threw a pillow at his head. "In case of you, and now I'm embarrassed."

Cillian got off the bed and reached into his wallet bringing out a wrapper. "I brought this in case my dreams came true."

"Your dreams?"

"Yeah, for in case that one I met in that club let me get in her knickers."

For that he got a second pillow thrown at him.

He picked them up and put them back on the bed and then I watched as he unwrapped a condom and placed it over his cock.

"Now, where were we?" He winked.

He jumped on the bed and I let out a girly scream. "You made me jump."

"I'm going to make you something." He said, as he parted my legs and laid between them.

My breath hitched as I waited for him to push inside me. When he did, it brought it all home that it was over with Chris and I was onto something new. Whether that was the guy here now, or another in the future. A different path had emerged and right now that destination appeared to be paradise.

He moved slowly inside me and back out, back and forth. We fit together perfectly, his body and mine. He captured my mouth with his once again. As our movements quickened and pressure built, it was hard to breathe with our lips locked together but I didn't want to stop kissing him. We stayed together until the very last moment when I felt the tremors build inside me and then he stopped thrusting before his own climax came bringing mine along with it.

We collapsed back against the bed, a tangle of limbs and sweaty flesh.

Satisfied and warm, I drifted off to sleep for a while in Cillian's arms. When I woke it had turned dark, the lights from the street lamps outside casting an amber glow over the room. The alarm clock at the side of the bed said it was 10:26 pm.

"Cillian." I whispered.

He moaned something unintelligible.

"Cillian." I repeated a little louder.

He opened an eye. "What time is it?"

"Almost half-ten and I'm starving. Do you want something because I'm going to order room service?"

He stretched, and I admired his taut physique as he did so. I wanted to dance my fingers down his pecs, along those abs and follow the happy trail.

"Sure. Can I have a look at the menu?"

As I went to pass it to him, he pulled me back down onto the bed. "How long do you think the food will take to come?"

"Longer than me." I smirked.

"So we'll order and then I want seconds of you." My stomach fizzed with excitement before it let out another loud rumble that made Cillian belly laugh.

We ate burgers and fries and I chatted about my journey here. It was so easy. In the back of my mind was the niggling feeling that I should have been feeling regret about jumping straight into bed with this guy. I should have been playing it cool instead, but the fact remained that I didn't give a damn. I'd had a thoroughly amazing time.

After eating we both showered which ended up taking a lot longer than if we'd have gone in separately and then Cillian got dressed while I put on my pyjamas.

"Well, look at you all sexy in your little check jammies."

"I've my fluffy bed socks to put on yet." I giggled.

"See, I'd let you warm your cold feet on me."

"If you stay I'll get no sleep whatsoever. Now I've been travelling, and then you've worn me out with all these sexcapades."

"Sexcapades." He nodded his head. "I like it."

"Now I need you to leave so I, and the neighbouring hotel patrons, can sleep. I will see you tomorrow if I'm still coming on your tour."

"Okay, well you have a lie in and a sightsee and I'll meet you at 2pm tomorrow afternoon outside the tourist information place."

He walked over to me and gave me a deep, lingering kiss. "I'll see you tomorrow, and we'll see if you can keep your clothes on around me then. It'll be a little embarrassing if you strip off in the centre of Dublin but I'm all for doing it alfresco."

I pointed to the door. "Out."

He moved away laughing and gave me a kiss on the cheek as he left. I went back to my bed and threw myself against the mattress. What a night! What an amazing night. I picked up my mobile. Now to tell my family and friends that I stayed in and ordered room service. It wasn't a lie was it?!

CHAPTER Ten

**It's the little things,
(and the not so little…)**

Anna

I got up and ate breakfast and then I went back to bed, lying there reading my kindle. With a cup of tea at my side, I relaxed, enjoying the feel of the towelling robe I'd found hanging in the wardrobe.

Cillian had texted me to say he'd got back home safely last night and then he'd sent two more texts this morning. Let's put it this way, I couldn't have shown them my mother.

I wandered down to the tourist information office after asking two people for directions, arriving fifteen minutes before the tour started. There he was, standing with a bright green flag with the tour company name on it. As his eyes searched the crowds and then fixed on mine, a great big smile broke out across his face and he raised a hand. I waved back.

He hugged me. "Why do I have to take these fekin eejits around when I just want to go back to bed with you?" He whispered in my ear.

"I want the tour, so I'm one of your fekin eejits. Now get ready to show me around the place."

"Okay, get ready to be bowled over once again by my charms."

I tilted my head at him. "Have you been kissing the Blarney stone a little too enthusiastically?"

"Only if you've changed your name." He winked.

I think I'd have found a walking tour with anyone else boring, but Cillian's enthusiasm poured out and he charmed everyone there. I couldn't fail to notice the young women elbowing each other then staring at him.

When the tour finished and everyone walked off, two women hung on for a moment until Cillian ran over to me and gave me a massive snog. I watched over his shoulder as one shrugged at the other and they walked away. I had to admit to feeling a little smug.

"Now, do you like steak?" He asked.

"I love it."

"Okay, follow me. We're going back to Temple Bar."

We ate in a fantastic steakhouse and then he took me to the Palace Bar which he said had great craic. They had musicians playing, and the atmosphere was amazing.

The night drew to a close and Cillian walked me back to the hotel. I felt like we'd been on a proper date and I didn't know what to expect now. Was he going home, or coming to my room?

"So, I didn't want to presume but I know tomorrow is the day you were supposed to be getting married..."

My face fell. In all the fun of the evening it had escaped my mind.

"So I wondered, seeing as I just so happen to have my toothbrush on me, if I could keep you company this evening? Then I'm here in the morning, where I happen to have the day off and can provide you with a whole slew of entertainment in order to make tomorrow an amazing day."

I drew my hand to my face, resting my chin on my thumb and placing my index finger over my lips. "Hmmm, let me think about that..."

Cillian picked me up and carried me inside the hotel entrance into the lobby before placing me down. "You thought yet?"

"I'll think better in my room. Race you. Last one there's a loser."

As the light filtered in through my window the following morning, I propped myself up against my headboard and thought about what I would have been doing now. What Tania would be doing now in my place. The hairdresser had been booked for ten am and the make-up lady for eleven. Me, my mum, and bridesmaids, would have had champagne to help quell my nerves. My dress would have been hung over the door, the photographer around taking photos of the preparation. My nails would have been manicured the night before. I looked at my hands and felt grateful that the French polish I'd had done was chipping off and that I didn't look wedding day perfect. Thinking about it, about the extensions that were going to be clipped in to help with the elaborate hairstyle I'd seen in a bridal magazine, it was all fake anyway. The hair, the nails. That wasn't me, who I really was. I didn't wander around trying to emulate a fairy princess and would have probably ended up looking like a drag queen. I could picture it now, the make-up stood thick off my face for the 'photos'. Suddenly, I realized I felt fine exactly where I was. In bed, with this warm body at the side of me. Even if it was snoring loudly. Then I pictured myself in a registry office, with Cillian at my side while I wore my jeans and a jumper.

"Morning."

I startled, both at his voice and because of my thoughts. Was this what they called a rebound?

Were my feelings exaggerated and amplified because of my situation?

"Top of the morning to ya." I said.

"You know we don't say that, don't you?"

"Well you should. I like it."

"Do you like this?" He said, pulling back the sheet to reveal his morning wood. Then he pulled me back down under the covers.

"So after breakfast I'm taking you to a museum."

"What? Can't we come back to bed? I don't want to go to a museum, they're boring."

"I'm going to prove you wrong, and no we can't stay in bed. You've worn my dick off, it needs a rest. Might have to see if the hotel has a first aid kit so I can bandage him up."

After what became brunch despite Cillian claiming injury, I reluctantly trailed beside him as we headed to the museum. As we pulled up in front of the brick built building with its green signs, I burst out laughing. "A leprechaun museum?"

"See. I told ya you'd enjoy it. It's the best museum in Dublin."

We bought tickets and waited for the next tour

to start.

He was right. I loved every minute. The tour guide was a master storyteller, and she enchanted me with Irish folklore while we moved from one room to the next. My favourite was a room filled with giant furniture so you became a leprechaun size yourself and I climbed on the furniture giggling. At times Cillian had to help me, the furniture was really high. He'd brought his camera, and he snapped pictures while I was captivated by my surroundings. I guessed having been before it wasn't as exciting for him, but I made him climb on a huge chair with me anyway.

"Oh my God, this is brilliant." I told him. "Thank you for bringing me here."

"I told you. You need to have faith in me. I know what I'm talking about."

"Yes, I'm very lucky to have met you." I said.

"You are." He winked.

"So what's next?" I squinted as the daylight hit my eyes after an hour spent in relative darkness.

"Food and then a trip to the Guinness factory. You didn't do that already, did you?"

Sadly that took my mind back to the last time I'd been here. "No, I didn't really get to do anything then."

"Come on then." He said.

We walked for a while looking for somewhere to eat and then I recognised the familiar branding of my favourite pizzeria. "You call Pizza Express, Milano's." I said.

"Now, what'ya talking about there, you've lost me."

I stopped outside the restaurant. "This is where I go to eat my favourite pizza. Only in Sheffield it's called Pizza Express."

"Well we like to take our time in Dublin and enjoy food, so that's probably why we called it somet'ing else. We eating here then?"

"Yes please."

From there we caught a bus to the Guinness Storehouse. The history of the making of Guinness wasn't so bad and we had a little taster during the tour, followed by a pint in the Gravity Bar with its 360 degree views of Dublin as it ended.

I was so busy enjoying my drink and chatting with Cillian that 2pm came and went without my even noticing. I finally looked at the clock at 2:48 pm.

"Thank you."

Cillian leaned closer. "What are you thanking me for?"

"The time came and went and I was too busy enjoying being here with you to even notice."

"Good. There's nothing to be gained by thinking

on that gobshite. Here, let's make a toast."

I raised my pint glass.

"Thanks for being a maggot, Chris, so I get the pleasure of this beautiful lady today. Here's to your future, the lovely Anna - without the gobshite in it. May you have all t'luck in the world, you deserve it."

He chinked my glass.

"Slainte."

I repeated it and then asked him what it meant. He clutched his stomach with laughter. "So it could have meant 'I have a really hairy box' but you just took me in good faith and repeated it?"

"Yes, I trust you, so don't let me down by saying it means something horrible."

"It means good health, or cheers."

"Phew."

"Do you mean that though? You trust me? Even after everything that went on with your ex?"

"You're not him and I don't want to judge my future life on what that gobshite," I used Cillian's turn of phrase, "did to me. You've given me no reason not to."

"That means a lot."

I finished up my pint. "I'm going to get my dad a souvenir from the gift shop. He likes a Guinness." I paused. "Although he likes whiskey more."

"We can do the whiskey tour Monday if you like? I have work in the morning but I'll be done by two."

"Yes please. I love whiskey."

"Sssh." He placed a finger over my mouth. "You can't say that in the Guinness building."

"Is it closed tomorrow?" I asked, wondering why we couldn't go then.

"Err, no, it's just there's a prior engagement tomorrow."

"Oh, what's that?"

"I always eat with my ma and da on a Sunday."

"Oh." I could hear the disappointment in my voice myself at not being able to see him.

"Do you not want to go?" He looked at me cautiously.

"I'm invited? To meet your parents?"

"You try to get away with it. My ma's threatened to come to the hotel t'meet you. She's desperate to meet the girl I apparently can't shut up talking about. The one she has to thank for her finally being able to get rid of me out of the family home."

"Really?"

"Really? And then I wondered if you'd like to ditch the Fleet for a night and come and see my place? The one you forced me into getting."

"I'd love to. Cillian?"

"Yeah?"

"Can we go back to my room now?"

"Souvenirs and then a taxi. Let's go." He grabbed my hand, and we headed downstairs.

CHAPTER Eleven

Meet the parents

Anna

I had missed calls from my mum and Jenny; and messages from both of them, Lesley, and a few other people who wanted to know how I felt on the day of my non-wedding. My mother's last text was a very terse 'Are you alive or has that Cillian murdered you like I said he would?' Maybe she was hoping if he had he'd be courteous enough to reply to her.

Cillian had gone home in the early hours of the morning as he said he wanted to give me some space, which I took to mean he'd remembered I was coming to his after his mothers and he needed to clean.

I'd slept and then woken up this morning to all these messages. My simple text to them all yesterday of, *I'm fine and having a lovely time*, obviously not good enough.

I sent a text back to my mum.

Sorry for the delay in reply, she took a long time to die.

The phone ran immediately after.

"Hey, Mum."

"Don't you 'hey, mum' me, lady, after that sarcastic text. Me and your dad were worried sick. We know what yesterday was supposed to have been and there you are in Dublin on your own. I've looked at the place on Google, there are a lot of bridges and water."

"Mother, the fact I've not married Chris is a cause for celebration, not suicide. I had a lovely day. I went to the Leprechaun Museum and the Guinness Storehouse."

"I don't think this is normal behaviour, Anna."

"What do you want me to do? Pretend wail down the phone? Say I can't live my life without him? He did me a favour, Mum. If he hadn't drunk dialled me I'd be married to him now - to a cheating scumbag. I've done all the being upset I'm going to do. Life's short and I'm going to make the most of it. I wasted six years on him, Mum. Six years! I'm not wasting another second."

"You've slept with him, haven't you? The Irish one."

"I'm not going to answer that."

"That's why you're not upset. This one's obviously taking your mind off it."

"He really is. He's very good company, and I'm meeting his parents today."

"You're doing what? That's a bit sudden, isn't it? Don't you be eloping. We need to meet this fella first."

I groaned. "Mum, I'm not eloping. I'm having a bit of fun. A holiday romance. Leave me alone."

"Well, keep in touch when you're not in the bedroom."

"Mother!"

"What's she doing in the bedroom?" My dad's concerned voice sounded from behind.

"Um, she's had a bit of an upset stomach." My mum lied. "She's fine now though."

My dad took the phone.

"Hello, love. Flights can do that to you. You got some Immodium?"

"I'm fine now, Dad, thanks. Hey, I'm going to a whiskey museum tomorrow. I'll bring you something back."

"All I need back is my daughter. Nothing else."

After speaking to them, I texted Lesley to tell her I was enjoying myself, and ignored the messages from the other few who were just ghouls, wanting to feed off my envisaged destroyed soul. I dialled Jenny.

"Hey there."

"Stranger! How did yesterday go?"

"Didn't even realise it had got to my wedding hour. I was too busy in the Guinness Storehouse." I caught her up on events.

"You slept with him? Was it good?"

"Well, I've repeated it several times since so you work it out."

"So where's he taking you today?"

"His parents house."

There was a silence. "His parents? What's going on, Anna? This is only a bit of fun, right?"

"I honestly don't know what it is. I'm just going with the flow."

There was a sigh. "Anna, its a rebound thing. You were jilted and this guy has given you an ear, and then an escape route away from the wedding. But you barely know him..."

"I was with Chris for six years and it looks like I barely knew him either." I said tersely.

Another silence weighed heavy.

"I'm sorry. I shouldn't be biting your head off. You're only concerned and I would be if you'd been the one jilted and gone off on a jolly. But seriously, I'm having a great time and I'm fine. I'm accompanying him to Sunday lunch with his parents because that's where he always goes on a Sunday that's all. It's nothing special. He's just taking a mate."

"Okay. I'm sorry too. I'm just worrying."

"So did it go ahead then? He didn't get cold feet?"

"It went ahead. One of Kian's mates and his wife went. They said it was just another wedding - boring."

"Well, good, at least that's closure on that part of my life."

"You liar, you hoped one of them did a runner, didn't you?"

I giggled. "Is that mean?"

"No, I hoped for the same. They deserve each other, Anna, and you deserve a shit ton of happiness, so go enjoy yourself, and your lunch, and I'll look forward to seeing you on Wednesday. If you can still walk, you've not shagged him enough."

I laughed and ended the call. Then I showered, went down to breakfast, and then returned to my room where I dressed in a pair of plain black trousers, a red tee and put a cardi over the handle of my holdall in case it got cold.

"See you tomorrow, hotel room." I said, closing the door behind me and I went down to wait in the lobby for Cillian.

Cillian's parents lived in a four-bedroomed end terrace in Phibsborough. He said they'd considered downsizing once he'd left but with the grandchildren staying so often they'd decided to stay put.

By the time we arrived, I'd got myself worked up into a right state. Sweat poured down my back, and my heart felt like it was about to thud out of my chest.

Cillian knocked and after a moment we heard footsteps. A female voice shouted "They're here," and then a woman with light brown hair, just like her son's, opened the door. His mum wore jeans and a stripy lightweight jumper. Her hair was short, and she wore make-up.

"Well, come in. Welcome to our house, Anna. It's lovely t'meet ya."

As I stepped in she smiled at me.

"Shall I take off my shoes?" I asked as I watched Cillian walk straight through.

"You're fine with those flats. These laminate floors are grand. Nice of you to ask though, not like that one. Never had any respect for the house. Used to jump on all the furniture like it was one of those kids activity centres."

Cillian popped his head around the door. "Are you telling Anna stories of my childhood already? She's not through the doorway yet."

His mum rolled her eyes. "I'm Aisling, come

follow me through to the living room seeing as my son's already abandoned you."

She led me into a neutrally furnished room with a massive brown leather corner sofa. Cillian was sitting next to his father, whose eyes were on the television. The guy looked up and jumped to his feet.

"Good to meet you, Anna. But what are you doing hanging around with this eejit?"

I laughed. Cillian's dad had a kind face which put me straight at ease.

"This television addict is Darragh." Said Aisling. "I'll just do all the prep for lunch while he sits with his feet up."

"Is there anything I can do to help?" I asked.

"Oh no. I was only joking wit'cha. Now can I get you a drink? Tea, coffee?"

"She'll be on the hard stuff if she's spending time with Cillian." Darragh drawled.

"Da, you'll be putting her off me."

"A cup of tea would be lovely please. Medium strength, milk, no sugar."

"Coming right up."

Dinner passed pleasantly. There was no mention of my non-wedding and I guessed that Cillian hadn't told them about it. They spoke fondly of their grandchildren and asked me lots of questions about my own family and my life back in Sheffield. I could see the question on the tip of his mother's tongue. It was in her expression, in the opening of her mouth where words didn't come out. Instead she'd take a drink. It happened a couple of times. The unspoken question. *What's the future for you and my son?*

Maybe she worried I'd take him away, back to Sheffield.

The answer was I had no idea. I wasn't thinking beyond this week. This was all I could manage right now.

"So, you're back away to Sheffield on Wednesday?"

She'd found a way to indirectly question me after all.

"I am. But I've loved every bit of my visit here and I'm sure I'll be back soon." I smiled at Cillian and he returned it. It wasn't a definite commitment, but it was all I was capable of at this moment in time. My answer was enough to satisfy Aisling.

"Another cup of tea, Anna?"

We bid farewell a couple of hours after lunch and set off for Cillian's apartment. It was a one-bedroomed apartment on the second floor. As we walked into his living room I was surprised by the amount of light that flooded in. There were patio doors that led out onto a tiny balcony, which looked over the residential area. Not the best view, but a nice touch to the apartment. There was a further window on the same wall and a small dining table was in front of that one. He'd placed a small black sofa against the back wall.

"This is lovely, Cillian."

"You think so? Let me show you the rest of the space and you can bring your bag through to the bedroom."

He took me next to a small, basic kitchen with beech coloured units. All the rooms came off a narrow hallway, and laminate flooring in a lighter wood colour ran throughout. Next he showed me a small, white furnished bathroom, and then finally through to his bedroom. Again there were neutral tones. His bedding was slate grey, with curtains to match. The bedroom was a decent size - large enough for a wardrobe, and a chest of drawers with a television on top.

He took my holdall from my hand and placed it at the left-hand side of the bed.

"That's your side." He winked.

"I think I need to test whether this bed will be acceptable for the evening or not." I smiled.

Time passed quickly after that.

The following day he took me to the Jameson

Distillery where I learned all about the process of whiskey making. After a tasting at the end, we left the tour and went to the bar with our drinks vouchers. While Cillian enjoyed a whiskey with ice, I had mine with ginger ale and lime.

"I'd love a chandelier like that." I said, pointing to one of the fittings over the bar area made with bottles of Jamesons.

"Well, I can't manage that, but I could buy you a keyring from the gift shop?"

Tuesday we went to Kilmainham Gaol. Then it was Tuesday night and as we got back to my hotel, I knew the conversation I'd been avoiding was imminent.

"Shall I stay tonight?" Cillian asked. He stood at my hotel room window looking out over the bustle of Temple Bar.

"Do you want to stay tonight?"

"Absolutely. My last night to sleep with you in my arms."

"Then stay. I want you to stay."

"What's next, Anna?"

I sat on the edge of my bed. "I honestly don't know, Cillian. My life is in Sheffield, always has been. I can come back here to visit again, but I guess we can only see what happens. You could come up to Sheffield sometime?"

Cillian's shoulders slumped. "Yeah, I could visit, but I love it here, Anna. I don't want to move. All my family is here. We're very close." He rubbed the scruff on his chin. "Also my photography course starts in September." He looked at me. "You could do that you know? You could come here and study like me. We have bars here you can work in."

I walked over to him and placed my arms around his neck. "Let's make the most of tonight and not worry about tomorrow, hey?"

"Okay, Anna." He said, but I knew it was far from okay.

When we got up the next morning, Cillian was due at work. He showered and dressed and then sat on the end of my bed.

"I will miss you."

"I'm going to miss you too."

"Promise to text me as soon as you're home?"

"I'll text you each leg of my journey so you know where I am."

He kissed me. "Bye, boomerang."

I tilted my head. "Now what are you talking about?"

"I'm sending you home, hoping you come straight back." He said.

CHAPTER Twelve

Is this love?

Cillian

The week had passed so quickly and then she was gone, taking her strange accent with her.

I missed her already, and she'd only been gone a couple of days.

Returning home to my empty apartment I felt flat. I turned down my friends who asked me to come out for drinks and to pull. I was only interested in one woman. So instead I played Whitesnake and sang along to the lyrics, especially the ones that said she had a hold on me.

But now she was back home.

Maybe I really was rebound guy - like my ma had warned me I could be. *'I hope not, son, but ya have to be wary'*.

There was no excitement when I woke in a morning. I went through the motions as I sang Molly Malone on my tours, hoping I'd see her walk through the crowds.

She answered my messages through Facebook with answers like **I'm out tonight with Jenny and I'll be back late**.

Excuses.

Maybe the sooner I accepted I was a rebound holiday fling and quit messaging the better.

But for me it had been love.

Instant love.

And she'd probably never know.

Anna

I didn't know what to say to Cillian on Facebook. I was home and miserable, walking about my rented home and wishing I was back with him. But that was stupid, wasn't it? I'd known him only through social media and one week's worth of company. You can't change your life on a whim can you?

I took extra shifts at the bar and threw myself into work, but I was miserable.

Sitting at home with a glass of wine, I realised why.

I felt like I'd left my heart in Dublin and I was back here without it.

Surely it wasn't possible?

It couldn't be, could it, after such a short amount of time?

Was this love I was feeling?

CHAPTER Thirteen

Boomerang

Anna

"Okay. I told myself to mind my own business, but I can't." Rachel threw her cloth onto the bar. "Anna, you've been miserable since you got back. What are you messing about at?"

I let out a large sigh. "I feel like I want to just up sticks and move to Ireland. Be with Cillian. But that's dumb, isn't it? I've spent one week with him."

"Well, for what it's worth I'm gonna give you my advice."

I looked at her and listened.

"Me and Evan pratted about for years. Wasted years because we didn't act on how we felt. When we got together, you know what happened. He proposed the day after. Now we're married. It could all go wrong but right now it's so very, very right, and

I'm pleased I took the leap to marry the former manslut because now he's all mine."

"You and Evan are fabulous together."

"We are. Now, you spent six years with that creep, Chris. Despite all those years you still didn't know what he was really like, so I don't understand why you're staying in Sheffield miserable when you have a chance to be happy out there in Dublin. If it goes wrong, come back. Why are you looking at 'What Ifs'? What do you want, Anna? Go get it, whatever it is."

"Are you trying to lose me one of my best bar staff?" Dan said, walking around from the back. He met my gaze. "Actually I agree with Rachel, and for that reason, you're fired."

"What?" I gasped.

"You're fired. But I'll write you a fabulous reference as long as your new place of employment is in Dublin."

I looked from one to the other of them and bit my lip.

"You're right. Why am I wasting my precious life worrying about things going wrong when they could go very, very right?"

I whipped off my bar apron.

"I have a new life to organise."

Anna: I've got to go away with work on a

course about beer. Apparently there's not much internet. Speak soon.

Cillian: When you get back we need to talk.

It's amazing how quickly you can pack up your life. I stored some things at my mum's and others I put into paid storage. My parents and Jenny thought I was insane but wished me luck. My mum told me she needed to meet Cillian as soon as possible if he was the one. Then I packed a couple of cases and booked a flight back out to Dublin. I booked a hotel room for the night again in case I needed it and I decided if it all went wrong I'd tour round the rest of Ireland for a couple of weeks and then see if there was a photography course I could start back home. Despite 'firing' me, Dan had said I always had a job at the Nag's Head if I needed it.

I arrived at the hotel at 1pm. I'd called the tour company and knew Cillian would end his tour at Molly's statue around 5pm.

So, I waited. Watching the clock and wondering if I was making a stupid mistake.

Then it was time to go.

I hid in the entrance of Superdry, and then I heard the beginning of 'Molly Malone' drifting down towards me. I strolled toward the crowd, hiding myself behind other shoppers until I got nearer and stood at the edge. Then I started singing at the top of my voice. It might have been a really romantic moment for some, but my strangled cat impression caused a couple of sniggers from the crowd. But it didn't matter, because Cillian stopped singing, ran towards me and kissed me like I was the air he needed to breathe.

"What are you doing here?"

By now some were still singing and others were watching us intently.

"I wondered if you'd like a girlfriend? Only, I thought I might stay. I can find work here and somewhere to live. If that's okay with you?"

Cillian clutched at my upper arms and stared into my eyes. "Okay with me? That's the best news I've ever had in my life, and you're staying with me in my apartment. I'm never being separated from you again."

We kissed again and as the surrounding crowd stopped singing to let out an almighty cheer accompanied by a round of applause, I knew I'd come home.

To Dublin's fair city.
To Cillian.

Epilogue

The Luck Maker

Two years later

Anna

"Oh, she looks the spit of you as a baby, Anna. The very same." My mum cooed at our daughter, who was just a few days old.

I smiled at my mum. Aisling had said something almost identical when she'd seen her, but that she was the spit of Cillian.

I didn't care who she looked like. She was just perfect.

The door banged.

"Where is my favourite lady?" Cillian shouted, holding the hugest pink teddy you've ever seen. It was a good job we now lived in a 3-bedroomed house near Aisling and Darragh.

"I'm here." I said then laughed as I'd been rightly relegated to second place the moment Cillian laid eyes on our baby.

He swept her from my mum's arms.

"How's my Molly been today?"

"She's been perfect, Daddy." I said.

Moving to Dublin had proved the best decision ever. Cillian and I had wed in a civil ceremony four months after I moved there, and I was expecting our baby just shy of a year later. We were both studying photography and planned to set up our own business. In the meantime Cillian had been working for a car sales company, using his Irish charm to earn a huge commission every month, and up to being seven months pregnant, I'd worked behind the bar in a quiet Irish pub with an amazing atmosphere.

It was strange. My first visit to Dublin had seemed a disaster, but it had turned out to be the start of a new, fantastic life. Because I'd met Cillian, who'd brought me nothing but good fortune. He was my soulmate, my baby daddy, my life.

My Luck Maker.

THE END

ALL ABOUT ANGEL

I like writing short sexy stories that get readers hot under the collar while also entertaining and hopefully making the reader laugh.

Keep in contact with me here at

www.facebook.com/angeldevlinauthor

Find your favourite authors in one place!

www.subscribepage.com/bookhangoverlounge

Join us in the Book Hangover Lounge for giveaways and goodies ... and the perfect place to recover from a long night with your latest book boyfriend!

Thank you!!!

Also By

geni.us/AngelDevlinAmazonPage

BANNED

LUCKED

HIS PERFECT MARTINI

Printed in Great Britain
by Amazon